Rooster Brother

Rooster Brother

by Nonny Hogrogian

MACMILLAN PUBLISHING CO., INC.
New York
COLLIER MACMILLAN PUBLISHERS
London

 Macmillan Publishing Co., Inc., 866 Third Avenue, New York, N.Y. 10022 • Collier-Macmillan Canada Ltd. • Library of Congress catalog card number: 73-8090. Printed in the United States of America.

10 9 8 7 6 5 4 3 2 1

Library of Congress Cataloging in Publication Data

Hogrogian, Nonny. Rooster Brother. [1. Folklore—Armenia] I. Title. PZ8.1.H723Ro 398.2'2'095662 [E]
73-8090 ISBN 0-02-743990-9

FOR OUR GENTLE MOTHERS

Rachel and Veron

Long ago in Adana there lived a poor widow
who had a son named Melkon.
He was small but he was very clever.

They had little to eat but on Melkon's name day, his mother decided to prepare a feast. She sent him to the bakery to have a rooster put in the oven for their supper.

While the rooster was cooking, little Melkon wandered
through a nearby field and picked some flowers for his mother. Then
he returned to the bakery for the rooster and started for home.

Three bandits who were watching him snatched the rooster from the small boy's hands and laughed as they ran off with his supper.

Little Melkon vowed to make them pay for what they had done.

The next day he saw the first bandit at the tailor shop. The bandit had stolen a suit and was having it refitted. Little Melkon overheard him say, "This fine suit was left to me by my dear dead uncle. Will you please have it ready for me at four o'clock tomorrow?"

At three o'clock the next day
little Melkon arrived at the tailor shop.

"I have come to pick up my master's suit," he said.
"He needs it now instead of at four."

"He's lucky I finished it in time," said the tailor,
and he gave the suit to Melkon.

At four o'clock the bandit arrived and asked for his suit. The tailor replied, "But your servant called for it at three."

The bandit cursed the tailor and as he turned to leave he noticed a note on the door. It said,

Rooster Brother was here.
He will strike again.

The next day little Melkon saw the second bandit enter the jewelry shop. He listened at the window.

"My father left me this beautiful watch but the chain broke as I snatched it from my pocket one day. Can you fix it for me by noon tomorrow?"

"Certainly," said the jeweler, and the bandit departed.

SAMUEL
JAMAKORDZIAN
JEWELER

The next day at ten minutes before noon, little Melkon arrived at the jewelry shop.

"My master sent me to pick up his watch," he said. "I hope you have repaired the chain."

"Yes," said the jeweler, "I just finished the job." And he gave the watch to Melkon.

At noon the bandit arrived. He was furious when he was told the watch had been given to his servant. As he left the shop he saw this note on the door:

Rooster Brother was here.
He will strike again.

A few days later little Melkon saw the third bandit leading a goose and followed him. Soon they arrived at the bandits' hideout and he listened to the three men talking.

"Where did you get that plump goose?"

"From the butcher. He'll never know the difference."

"We'll have it roasted tomorrow for the All Thieves' Day feast."

The next day little Melkon was waiting and watching near the bakery. The bandits left the goose to be roasted and went to the baths.

Melkon went too. He took their pants and in their place he left a note,

Rooster Brother was here.
He will strike again.

Then he went back to the bakery and picked up the goose
and left a note on the door,

Rooster Brother was here.
He will strike again.

And so little Melkon and his mother had their feast after all,
and the bandits, who had had enough of Rooster Brother,
left Adana and never returned.

The End